CALLING
the

WHALES

JASBINDER BILAN

Illustrated by
SKYLAR WHITE

Stoke

First published in 2023 in Great Britain by
Barrington Stoke Ltd
18 Walker Street, Edinburgh, EH3 7LP

www.barringtonstoke.co.uk

Text © 2023 Jasbinder Bilan
Illustrations © 2023 Skylar White

A CIP catalogue record for this book is available
from the British Library upon request

ISBN: 978-1-80090-180-3

Printed in Great Britain by Charlesworth Press

For Satchen and Gem,
my little conservationists

CHAPTER 1

It's night-time. Satchen and I are standing at the foot of the Craig – an ancient volcanic hill. It towers above us, stretching away towards the stars. We shouldn't be here so late, but then rules are made to be broken – right?

"Race you to the top!" I yell. I playfully push Satchen, my best friend.

"Hey! That's not fair, Tulsi," Satchen complains to me. "You're already way ahead."

"Catch up then," I say. "Put some power into it!"

I scramble off into the darkness and begin scaling the giant hill of grassy rock. We've both climbed the Craig so often, from the minute we could walk.

The moon is full and sends its light sparkling around us.

"I'm going to be a sky runner like Mira Rai," I shout, "scaling the steepest mountains, running up the highest peaks in the world. I'll climb Ben Nevis at night, maybe even Mount Everest!"

"Ahh, slow down," says Satchen.

I get to the top of the hill first. Satchen's heavy breaths behind me mix with the ghostly sounds of the seabirds. I reach for his hand and pull him up beside me. "We did it!" I yell. "We got to the end of Primary Seven – summer holidays and high school here we come!"

From the top of the hill I can see everything. There's the glow of fire coming from the steelworks on the other side of the estuary. Our little town, East Shawle, with its harbour and the fishing boats bobbing against the wall. The sea is the colour of lead, moving like a monster with white frothy hair. And beyond that is the island with the tiny lighthouse perched high on one side. The island is our special place – where

Satchen and I can be wild and free. I breathe in the salty air until it reaches right inside my lungs. I stare into the sky with its trillions of stars.

I take a few steps backwards and twist round. Now I'm facing the whale monument next to us on the hill. The huge whale's jawbone is lit up and casts a spooky shadow across the glistening grass. I've seen it so many times before but tonight the moon makes it look more dramatic than ever.

"Can you believe this used to be an *actual* whale's jawbone?" I say, touching the bone. "Before they replaced it with this replica."

"I know," says Satchen. "The fact they'd ever use a real bone makes me so sad. I never want any whales to be killed ever again."

"Agreed. Do you think the ghost of the whale still haunts the Craig?" I ask.

"Maybe," says Satchen, leaning against the whale's jawbone.

"If I were the whale," I continue, "I think I'd stay around to protect the waters. I mean, there are so many dangers for whales these days."

The sea far below us suddenly churns. Its ripples glint against the moonlight and the smell of fresh salt blows towards us on a flurry of cold wind. The moon shines even more brightly, lighting up the whole of the bay.

"Imagine what it was like in the old days," I say, "before we had the chance to spoil the seas with all the rubbish that gets washed up. There was nothing in the water apart from sea creatures and plants."

"That's why we have to keep going with our work," says Satchen. I can hear the determination in his voice. "We can't wait around for the adults to take action. It's up to

us. As my dad says, we can do anything if we put our minds to it."

"It always feels like there's so much to be done," I say. "It does feel good when we do a beach clean or sponsored run or walk. But can we really make a difference?"

"We raised £500 last year, Tulsi," says Satchen. "That's a lot. Hopefully we'll be able to raise even more once we're in high school as it's a much bigger school."

"What's that?" I ask, pointing way across the water to where the ripples on the sea are shimmering in the darkness.

"I don't see anything," replies Satchen. "It's just the wind, I think ... or the ghost of the old whale." He elbows me lightly in the ribs.

"Stop it," I tell him. "There could be ghost whales. You never know."

"We'd better get back before we're missed," says Satchen. "Mum sometimes checks up on me in the middle of the night – after the last time she found my bed empty." Satchen kicks at the ground. "She seems to worry about everything now."

"Sorry," I say, touching his arm. "How's Isla?" Isla is Satchen's baby sister. She was born a few weeks ago but is back in hospital.

"Not much better," Satchen says. He looks back across the sea. "But not worse." He pauses. "Mum says Isla is like a baby chick come too soon. Her bones are still soft and she needs some time to make herself strong. The last time she was home I spent all night with Mum, sitting beside Isla's cot. She's got a grip on her." He smiles. "She wouldn't let my pinkie go."

"That means she's a survivor – she wants to stay," I say.

"She liked my wee lullabies."

"She can't complain about your singing yet," I tease.

"Oi," says Satchen, pretending to be offended.

"My granny's got a book at home," I tell him. "It's full of Hindu gods and goddesses. Honestly, you wouldn't believe it. They're amazing. Full of all sorts of powers. Granny lights her candles and prays to the gods and goddesses for good things to happen. I'll get her to say some prayers for Isla." Then I get another idea. "Let's say a prayer to the whale ... in case it *is* watching over us."

Satchen gives me a look that says, *What wild thoughts you have, Tulsi.* But I don't care.

"Dear whale," I begin, "if your spirit is still here, please protect Isla, Satchen's baby sister, and make her strong. And help us to protect our planet by bringing us extra luck with our fundraising."

Satchen's eyebrows crinkle together as if he's not sure any of this will work.

"It might help," I say. "It's worth a try."

We stand together for a moment and Satchen says, "Thanks for bringing me up here. We haven't done it in ages but it always makes me feel better."

"On the Craig I feel like we're part of something bigger," I say, looking up at the stars.

Across the sea the moon shines on the waves and I see the ripples rising again. "Look, Satchen," I say. "Can't you see? Don't you think the water looks strange tonight?"

He squints towards the island. "The water's churned up. It's hard to see but I think it's just the full moon making the tides change."

"Let's go down to the beach," I say, "and take a proper look."

"What if Mum checks in on me?" asks Satchen. "It's not fair to make her worry again."

"Sorry, you're right. Let's get back."

We leave the whale's jawbone behind and hurry down the Craig. Moonlight casts spiky shadows ahead of us and owls hoot in the woods below.

Once we're at the bottom, I squeeze Satchen's arm. "Try not to worry – Isla will be OK."

He forces a smile and I watch him for a moment as he heads towards his home. It's one of the old fishermen's cottages close to the harbour.

I'm about to run home too but I can't get the rippling image of the sea out of my head. It's as if something is pulling me towards the beach, wanting me to go there, so I do.

The beach is lit up by the moon. It floods the sea with magical light as the waves shush softly onto the sand. Everything's calm, everything's normal. But I can't shake the feeling that something's happening out there in the waters around our island. The thought sends shivers into my chest as I turn and head for home.

CHAPTER 2

"I'll be out all day," I say at breakfast the next morning. "Me and Satchen are going to the island."

I'm not allowed my phone at the table but it's balanced on my knee. I tap a sneaky message to Satchen:

Meet by the boat – something exciting's going on.

I manage to ping it off before Mum and Dad see.

Mum frowns. "I don't like you rowing all that way by yourselves," she says.

"Promise us you'll be careful," says Dad.

"You worry too much," I say, shoving my cereal bowl in the dishwasher. "We've rowed there hundreds of times. Nothing's ever happened so far."

I collect supplies, push them into a rucksack and give Mum and Dad a kiss. "See you later," I say.

I run fast along the high street. The feeling I had last night makes my stomach flip with possibility. I pass the paper shop, where Mr Macdonald rattles the blue shutters open, and Tiddlers Nursery with its striped bunting waving in the breeze.

I arrive at the harbourside and Satchen's already there. The sky is milky blue and the summer breeze ruffles his red hair.

"What's the hurry? I was having a lie-in," he says, yawning.

"Last night after you left, I came down to the beach," I say. "I think something's going on – out there." I shield my eyes against the sun and stare towards the island.

"Come on then," Satchen says, throwing his things into the boat, named *Shona*. "Let's take a look."

We untie the heavy wet rope and drag the boat down to the shore. We both climb in and the curved green sides bob against the waves. Salt water washes the final grains of sand away from the painted boat.

"Remember when we rescued her?" I say.

"We brought her back to life, didn't we?" Satchen replies.

"And gave her a new name," I say. "*Shona*, queen of the sea!"

I take the oars and dip them in the clear emerald waters. Black-and-white guillemots whistle alongside us.

"How's Isla?" I ask, pushing the oars against the waves.

"Dad was with her all night at the hospital. He said he's sure she gave him a wee smile when he left."

"Isla will be home before you know it," I say.

Satchen crinkles his eyes at me but I can tell he's still worried.

*

I watch the shoreline get further away until we're surrounded by sea in all directions.

Satchen and I take turns guiding the boat and rowing until the island gets bigger.

As we get closer, I hear a strange noise, almost like the cry of a baby.

Satchen's eyes pop wide.

"What do you think it is?" I say.

"It sounds so weird," he replies, digging the oars in deeper.

"Do you think it's coming from the island?" I ask, shivers shooting along my spine.

"I don't know," says Satchen. "It's stopped now."

The air is eerily still.

"Row faster," I breathe.

"Or row back," says Satchen. His eyebrows join together like caterpillars.

I ignore him. "There's something odd going on," I tell him. "I felt it last night and again now. We can't turn back. We have to find out what it is."

The top of the abandoned lighthouse juts into the sky above the island as Satchen hauls us closer. His knuckles are white as he grips the oars too hard. Just as he brings the boat into shore, we hear the strange crying sound again.

We're both tired from the effort of the journey, so we drag the boat onto the beach and collapse on the warm sand beside it.

I grab some water from my rucksack and offer it to Satchen. He takes three thirsty gulps, then hands it back.

"You can walk the whole island in around an hour," Satchen says. "So if there is something here, we'll soon find it."

The thought sends butterflies fluttering inside my belly.

"It could just be the sound of the wind," he continues. "Or the birds – half of them sound like squawking babies."

I stare over at the grey rocks. They're covered in all sorts of seabirds. "You might be right," I say, "but let's see."

We put on our rucksacks and leave the boat safely moored on the sand. Then we set off in search of whatever it was that made the heart-stopping cry.

Heading in the direction of the lighthouse, we clamber over steep rocks tufted with rough grass. Soon we're on the other side of the island where the wind blows wilder.

We stand high above the beach, the giant sand dunes rolling down to the shoreline.

"Do you think there's something down there?" I ask, squinting towards the cliff on the far side of the beach.

"I think we should take a look beyond the cliff," Satchen replies. "It's the only part of the island we can't see. Then we can relax and have our sandwiches before heading back."

That feeling I had before of my stomach caving in on itself has come back. I don't know why but a sense of dread is making my feet freeze to the spot.

"I – I don't know," I say, knowing I sound like a coward.

"You were the one who wanted to find out what the sound was, so let's go," Satchen says.

"You're right – come on then."

We rush down the dunes, our feet sinking into the soft crumbly sand until we reach the beach.

And that's when we hear the sound again. This time there's no mistake. It's coming from the other side of the cliff, from the sheltered cove beyond.

My heart pumping, I move closer to Satchen and together we walk in the direction of the haunting cry.

CHAPTER 3

The sun disappears behind the clouds, casting our shadows ahead of us, pointing towards the hidden cove.

"What will we do if it's a monster?" asks Satchen, dragging his feet across the wet sand.

"It's not going to be a monster." Even as I say this, memories of all the monsters from all the horror films I've ever seen flash into my mind. Fear tugs at my insides.

Satchen grabs me by the hand. "Let's hurry up and find out what it is."

We make our way closer to the cove, our feet sinking into the sand. Soon we're standing below the tall cliffs that rise up towards the clouds. We continue onwards and reach the cove at last, standing on the curve of beach, the cliff behind us now.

The sea is darkest grey, the waves slapping softly onto the shore. Out in the near distance there's something in the deeper water, something huge and lumbering, but I can't work out what it is.

I stand on the shore, staring out, trying to decide what it can be.

My heart begins to pound. And now I see it clearly as the salt water parts over the top of it and pushes back towards the sea.

"It's a whale!" I cry. "An actual whale."

"But what's it doing here?" asks Satchen, his face full of disbelief.

"They can get lost," I say, "confused by all the sounds of boats' sonar and stuff." I feel my heart thrumming loudly beneath my ribs. "But it's too close to the shore."

"The whale must be stranded, Tulsi."

In the distance the waves wash backwards and forwards over its huge grey body, covering it in salt water, protecting it.

"This was what I could see from the top of the Craig," I say.

"It must have been separated from its family," says Satchen, "and swum into shallow waters."

"What are we going to do?"

"It's not like we can call for help," says Satchen. "There's no signal out here."

"We have to do something," I say, full of passion. "Let's swim out to it. At least that way the whale will know it's not alone."

"OK," agrees Satchen. "We're both strong swimmers and the currents on this side of the island aren't dangerous."

We change into our wetsuits in a hurry and stow our rucksacks away from the water.

We don't care about the freezing cold as we rush into the peppermint green sea. Long strands of slimy seaweed touch my face but I keep moving forwards, towards the shape in the water.

With each stroke I take, the salty sea rises up and covers my head. It stings my eyes, goes up my nose, but all I can think of is that we have to get to the whale.

I keep pushing my arms and legs against the waves, taking shallow breaths in and out. At last we reach the spot where the whale is floating.

The creature is huge, even bigger than I imagined. It's about the length of twelve school tables pushed together. I hold my head above the water as the sun shines along its grey body, sparkling on the ridges along its flippers.

I know other people have seen humpback whales around here but this is my first time. A feeling of fear and wonder snaps at my insides.

My muscles are tired and I'm out of breath but I know I have to stay strong. I tread water beside the whale, my fingers and toes so numb I can't feel them any more.

The whale makes a sharp sound that's so haunting and distressing, a deep feeling of dread fills every part of me.

I lift my hand and press it to the whale's side, trying to soothe it. The sun casts watery shadows across the whale's back and its eye looks straight into mine. I swallow the lump in my throat and put my face against its head.

"We're here to protect you," I whisper. "We won't let anything bad happen … I promise. Don't be scared."

I know how difficult it has been to help other whales that have swum too close to shore. There have been many times when rescuers had to bury the whales as they couldn't save them.

"Tulsi, look," says Satchen. He's tugging at something floating like seaweed around the whale's body.

"It's part of a fishing net," I cry, water filling my mouth.

"The whale's all tangled up and can't swim free," Satchen continues.

I stroke the whale's face. "We're going to help," I say.

But my energy is fading, the cold sea sucking it from me.

"Let's swim back," whispers Satchen. "I'm getting tired – we can work out what to do once we reach shore."

"We'll be back," I whisper to the whale. "Promise."

We swim away slowly, pulling ourselves through the waves until we're back on land.

I throw myself onto the sand, blood pumping in my ears. I'm weak from the effort. I look back to sea – the whale's body makes a shadowy shape against the sunlight. I think of the sounds it was making, the way it looked at me, and I send it a message:

Stay strong – help is coming!

I clutch Satchen's arm. "We have to think of a plan," I say, "and quick!"

CHAPTER 4

Satchen delves into his rucksack and brings out sandwiches and a flask of hot chocolate. "Here," he says. "You must feel like an iceberg too. This'll warm us up."

I take the steaming cup with shaking hands and wrap my fingers around it. "You're the best," I say, taking a bite of the sandwich. My body feels floppy and I'm not sure if I have the strength to swim back out to the whale, let alone try to rescue it.

"Do you think it's a boy, a girl or a they?" I ask.

"What?" mumbles Satchen, his mouth crammed with bread. Then he says, "I think it's only males that sing."

"We should give him a name then," I reply. "That way we can make a deeper connection with him. It'll help him stay strong."

"What's a good whale name?" Satchen asks, glugging down the hot chocolate.

"What about Angus?" I suggest. "In Celtic mythology he's the god of youth and love."

Satchen nods in agreement.

"Now all we have to do is save Angus," I say. "I brought my knife. We can use it to cut away the rope and nets."

"Come on," says Satchen. "We'll row out to Angus in the boat. That way we can rest when we get tired."

"We have to work as fast as we can," I say. "We don't know how long he's been stuck like that."

The food and drink has given us energy and we hurry back to the boat on the other side of the island. We push out into the sea and begin rowing round the shoreline towards Angus.

"Show me the fastest route round the rocks," I say, pulling hard at the oars. "We can't waste a second."

Satchen fixes his gaze ahead and begins shouting out directions as he guides us forward.

"We're coming, Angus," we both call over the sound of the birds.

The breeze has picked up, turning the waves choppy. It's hard work but we take turns to pull the boat through the water. At last we're almost round the other side of the island.

It's as if Angus knows we're here, coming to save him, and he lets out a long call.

We keep going, pushing away from the island and further out to sea until we reach the spot where Angus is floating. The tangled mess of plastic rope and netting has wound itself around one of his fins, fixing Angus to the spot.

"Let's take turns in the water," says Satchen as he drops the anchor. "That way we can gather our energy and rest between each dive."

"Good plan," I reply. Hands shaking, I pull on my mask and snorkel, find my knife and tuck it into the elastic of the mask. "I'll go first."

I take a deep breath and dive underwater, plunging myself into the rough swirling waves. I kick my legs hard behind me, searching for the netting that's bound itself around Angus.

I get close to Angus's slick body and yank hard at the tough plastic strands of the net.

I begin to saw back and forth with the sharp knife.

I can only last a minute at most, as the water is pushing its way down into the snorkel. But I surface to take another deep gulp of breath and go back – again and again. Each time I manage to cut a little more.

I grip the side of the boat. "There's so much netting," I say, stopping to rest.

"I've been singing to Angus," says Satchen. "He seems to like it. He's been making these clicking sounds, like he's talking to me, telling me all about his sea journeys."

I give Satchen a weak smile as he helps me back into the boat. I feel myself trembling from the cold and from being in the water so long.

"Wish me luck," he says, taking the knife from me and diving in.

I cocoon myself tight in the blanket from my rucksack but I still can't stop shivering. My lips are so cold I can barely move them to sip the hot chocolate from the flask.

"S-so Satchen's been singing to you, has he?" I stutter to the whale. I lean out of the boat and touch Angus's barnacled skin. "Did you like it?"

He makes the clicking sounds Satchen told me about and I gaze at him in wonder. "I bet you've seen so much with these eyes of yours. Have you got family out there, missing you? They must be looking for you."

I finish the final dregs of the hot chocolate in my cup and feel a little warmth return to my blood.

"Are you OK?" I call as Satchen bobs out of the water like a red-headed seal.

He nods. "I'm going down again. There's a lot of netting and it's twisted tight in places, but you did a good job of loosening it. I've managed to cut quite a bit."

Angus lets out a piercing cry again.

"You must be so desperate to be free," I say to Angus as I watch Satchen disappear back under the waves. The current is getting stronger. I cross my fingers tight, hoping Satchen can cut more of the rope that I managed to loosen.

My voice is way rougher than Satchen's but, still, I think a song might help Angus to know how hard we're trying.

I begin singing the lullaby "Little Fishes". It's what my mum used to sing to me when I was little. "When the houses lie in darkness, when the humans sleep in bed ..."

I sing badly and stroke Angus's skin. By some miracle he seems to respond. At least he's not making the pitiful cry like before and he's started with the clicking sounds again. They almost seem to be joining with my song, so I carry on.

"Then the people of the sea, leave their homes and head for land ..."

After a while, Satchen appears beside the boat again. His face is pale, almost blue.

"Quick," I cry, helping him in. I pour him a hot drink clumsily. "Here, get this down you." I throw the other blanket around Satchen's shoulders. "How did you get on?"

"I managed to make a few cuts," he says, teeth chattering. "The rope's really tough and my hands are covered in blisters."

I can see he's exhausted but I don't know if I have the energy to go back in the water again. When I swipe my cheeks, they're wet with tears. "I'm sorry, ignore me. I'm just getting tired," I tell him.

"Maybe we should go to get help," Satchen says, frown lines across his brow. "We're just kids and the only thing we've got is that penknife."

"Thinking like that isn't going to help Angus," I say.

"I'm so tired, Tulsi," Satchen continues. "I don't think I can go on."

"Come on, Satchen, what's got into you?" I say, and move closer. "We're the only hope Angus has got – we can't let him down."

"You're right," Satchen says, looking out to sea. "Sorry for being so negative."

While we've been busy trying to free Angus, the day has flitted away like a seabird. The red ball of sun has moved over to the west and grey clouds are hurrying across it.

We both notice the change in weather at the same time. The clouds are darkening and heavy with rain. Satchen tucks the blanket further round himself.

And now my tears come thick and fast.

"There's a storm coming," I howl.

CHAPTER 5

The first crack of thunder is faint. The sky suddenly darkens as the black storm clouds shift together like a sky monster.

Satchen begins to bundle the blanket away into his rucksack and grabs for the oars. "We need to get back to shore and we need to be quick."

"But Angus isn't free yet," I say. "We can't just run away and leave him!"

"You know it's not safe. We've done what we can," Satchen says.

The second crack of thunder is louder, followed by a streak of lightning that fills the sky with a blinding glow.

I'm about to get back into the water but Satchen grabs hold of my sleeve.

"I have to give it one more try," I say, shaking him off. I grip my knife and get ready to dive back in.

"Don't be so stubborn, Tulsi," Satchen says. "This is serious. We have to get to safety."

I fold my arms across my chest. "I don't want to leave Angus."

"We can't waste time arguing about it," says Satchen, shivering. "We need to go back and get help."

The first splat of cold rain splashes my cheek and brings me back to my senses. "You're right," I say. A tight knot of fear twists my stomach. "Come on then, let's get going."

"We're not going to abandon you, Angus," says Satchen, and gives the whale a final encouraging look. "We'll be back."

The rain comes hard and fast now, pelting us with freezing drops. We lift the anchor and turn our little boat away from Angus, back towards home and help.

Above us the storm begins to whirl like an angry god. I feel so tiny in this vast sea-storm. Satchen and I squeeze close on the seat of the boat and take an oar each. We pull on them together, trying to get the boat to move through the water. But the weather is changing so fast and the waves are lifting higher and higher, splashing big bucketfuls of water into our boat.

*

We struggle against the waves for as long as we can. I've no idea how much time passes. But it feels as if we're being pulled away from shore rather than making any progress.

Satchen's face is as pale as paper, cold rain drenching him. "This is pointless," he says, his lips trembling. "I don't know if I can do it any more."

"You're just tired," I say, shouting to be heard above the sound of the wind. "But we can't give up. We have to keep heading home. Angus is relying on us and we can't let him down."

From somewhere we find a new surge of energy and dip the oars back into the sea. It has turned the colour of darkened stone. The boat rocks violently on the waves and we're trying hard to keep rowing in a straight line but the boat seems to have a will of its own.

Suddenly a huge wave hits the side of the boat, knocking Satchen off the seat. He loses his grip on the oar and it splashes into the water. The sea swallows it like a hungry animal.

My heart plummets. It was hard enough to make any progress with two oars. With one it's going to be hopeless.

My throat tightens. I lean forward and grip Satchen's arm. "Are you OK?" I ask.

"I'm just feeling so cold and tired, Tulsi," he says in a whisper.

"Just rest," I tell him. "You're going to be fine."

There's nothing much I can do to make Satchen feel better when I'm feeling so hopeless myself but I give his arm a squeeze.

Satchen has closed his eyes. Even in the hammering rain I can see his cheeks are blazing red.

I take the single oar and try my hardest to grip my frozen fingers around it and row. But the waves are too strong and, as much as I try, my paddling is making no difference. I'm just turning us round in circles.

I sit for a while feeling helpless as we're tossed around in the waves. I'm sure I can see the clouds lightening a little in the distance. But just as I start to feel hopeful that the storm might be easing, a whip of wind lashes against us and tips the boat over with a loud slam. Everything goes into a frantic spin.

Seawater funnels up my nose. "Satchen!" I scream. "Hold on to the boat."

I throw my arms against the icy sea and somehow we find each other. Linking arms tightly, we hold on to the rough timbers of the boat as best we can. There's no way we can

turn the boat over to get back inside. So we dig our fingernails into the wood.

The storm whirls around us, pushing us in and out of the water, hard rain beating down on our backs.

"Are you OK, Tulsi?" asks Satchen in a low voice. "Will someone find us?"

"I don't know," I murmur as I try desperately to keep my eyes open.

CHAPTER 6

Time seems to stand still as we float on the vast wild sea. I've lost all sense of direction, clinging to the boat as the weather swirls around us.

At some point I hear another noise over the sound of the storm. It vibrates through the waves and suddenly I catch sight of something coming towards us, against the rain.

"It's Angus," I cry weakly. "He's come to save us."

"What?" says Satchen, opening his eyes. "Did we free him?"

"I think so."

In the beating rain, Angus swims our way – the most beautiful sight, bringing us hope at last. He comes alongside us and nudges the boat forward. We use our last bit of strength to scramble further onto the overturned boat.

Angus must be weak from the time he's spent tangled up in the fishing gear, yet I feel his power and strength as he beats against the storm. He pushes us through the never-ending high waves.

Satchen and I are both beyond tired, our bodies like limpets stuck to the bottom of the boat. But the noises that Angus makes are as soothing as a lullaby and he continues to push us along.

As I drift in and out of consciousness, I dream that Satchen and I are actually riding on his strong back. Nothing matters now. Angus is taking us on an adventure across all the oceans of the world, showing us its treasures and wonders.

*

At last the storm blows over and the night sky above fills with stars. The wind has died down and now billows about us gently. Angus glides in the water more easily.

"Can you believe this?" I whisper.

Satchen's eyes are wide with amazement.

I know I should feel frightened as I have no idea how we're going to get home, but all I can think is that we did it. We actually saved Angus. It's a moment in time that I'll remember for ever, a story I can tell Mum and Dad when I see them. Maybe I'll tell it to my children and my grandchildren too – the day I saved a whale and dreamed of riding the oceans on his back.

And then in the light of the full moon I see something in the distance – a boat!

"Satchen, look!" I say.

He lifts his head and gives a faint smile.

I strain my eyes to look at the boat. We must have floated further out to sea than I thought. I don't see the lights of East Shawle,

just an orange searchlight – it's a lifeboat, skimming the surface of the grey sea like an early morning sunrise.

My energy is almost gone but I won't give in to sleep. I keep my eye fixed on the dot of the lifeboat in the distance and will it to move faster.

As the boat draws nearer, I hear Mum's worried voice reaching out to us over the Tannoy.

"Tulsi? Satchen?" Mum repeats again and again.

Angus must sense that he's done his job and he brushes past us. I stroke his barnacled skin one final time. He comes close and I press my face against his, staring into his wondrous eye that's full of mystery and bravery.

"Safe travels, dear Angus – and thank you," I say. My mouth is parched and my skin feels leathery and weather-worn but a feeling of happiness floods my body.

*

Once the lifeboat finds us, the rescuers haul us from the water and get us on board as fast as they can.

I hear Mum's voice again. "But … a whale?"

Everything is a blur. I think I hear Satchen's dad but I'm not sure.

I feel the slippery foil sheet and the heavy blanket as they're wrapped around me. Mum and Dad are beside me and I feel safe at last.

I look out to sea one final time. Way off in the distance, Angus is swimming away. But he's not alone.

I tug at Satchen's blanket and say, "Look."

There are one, two, three whales. They're humpbacks like Angus. I see him rise from the surface of the water and leap into the air. He lands against the waves and makes a loud vibrating sound that reaches us.

"It's Angus's family here to take him home,"
I say.

All Satchen can do is nod but a broad smile
lights up his tired face.

Now that we're safe, a cloud of exhaustion
comes over me, forcing my eyes closed. All I
feel is the bobbing of the water surrounding me
and imagine Angus's barnacled skin beneath
my fingertips. I dream of him swimming the
oceans with his family and the sun beating
down on his back. I send them a message of
love.

*

When I finally wake up, I'm back at home in
my bedroom.

Mum's sitting on a chair beside me and
when I open my eyes, she jumps up straight

away. She takes my hand in hers and strokes it gently.

"You've been asleep for days, my darling," Mum says.

She has dark circles around her eyes and her face is puffy.

"What happened?" Mum asks, then bursts into tears. "We were so worried, Tulsi."

"We found a stranded whale," I say, sitting up slowly. My lips are cracked and it's hard to speak.

"Take a sip of this." Mum puts the rim of a mug against my lips and helps me to drink. "It's a special soup to help you recover."

"Is Satchen OK?" I ask. I can't really remember what happened at the end.

"He's recovering too," says Mum, smiling. "And baby Isla's home for good. Amazingly, the whole time you were missing she was getting stronger."

"I'm sorry, Mum," I say. "I didn't mean to make you worry. But once we found the whale, we couldn't just leave him. We called him Angus and he was trapped in fishing gear. He couldn't move. We cut him free."

"It was incredible, Tulsi," Mum says. "We saw what the whale did. He brought you to safety." She puts an arm around me. "But don't get over-excited – you need to rest." Mum wipes her cheek. "We're just so happy you weren't injured after all that time in the storm."

"So Angus really did save us," I say. "I wasn't sure if I dreamed that part. Did you see his family too?"

"Yes," soothes Mum. "Everyone saw them."

"Whales are getting caught in fishing gear. It has to stop."

I get a vision of Angus caught in the ropes and net. The unfairness of it makes my heart hammer against my chest.

"Once I'm better, Satchen and I have to go to the papers and tell our story," I say. "We have to stop this happening again."

"OK, OK," says Mum, putting the duvet back round me. "But for the moment, it's time for more rest."

CHAPTER 7

Mum and Dad make me stay in bed for ages. They say I've been through a huge ordeal. They keep the curtains half closed even during the day so I can rest and build my strength.

But at last I'm well enough to leave my room. A few weeks after it all happened, we make our way back to the top of the Craig. Back to the place where it all started.

Reporters and photographers from the *East Shawle Daily* are milling about taking photos of the view and the whale's jawbone.

Satchen's been allowed to carry his wee sister Isla, bundled in the baby carrier. He shuffles a few steps towards me.

I take Isla's little fist and she wraps it tight around my pinkie. "Hello there," I say. "Look, she's smiling at me! I think she knows me already."

"I think she likes you," Satchen laughs, and Isla makes a cute squawking noise like a baby bird.

Isla has red hair like Satchen and his dad. Fine wisps poke out from the green knitted bonnet covering her head.

"I'm so happy Isla is out of hospital," I say, stroking her skin that feels as soft as down.

"Me too," agrees Satchen. "Mum and Dad are still a bit jittery about her. They watch her like hawks, even when she's sleeping."

"Can we get a photo of the heroes?" one of the photographers calls.

Satchen gives Isla to his dad and the two of us stand in front of the whale's jawbone for the photos.

Next it's the turn of the radio presenter. She's come all the way from Edinburgh to interview us.

"Whales have always been part of the history of this area of Scotland," the presenter begins. "We're standing under the gaze of the famous whale's jawbone perched on top of the Craig in East Shawle. It was out there in the North Sea that two local youngsters risked their lives to save a whale. Satchen and Tulsi, what's your message to anyone listening?"

"Satchen and I got into difficulty because we were trying to save a whale that had got caught up in a fishing net," I say. My nerves are making my palms sweat. "But in the end the whale managed to get free and he saved us. Lots of other animals aren't so lucky. Fishing gear in the sea is a huge threat to wildlife." I try to speak more confidently as I add, "You can raise awareness about the issue by writing to your MP asking for laws to be put in place to protect sea-life."

"Yes," agrees Satchen. "The huge nets used to catch fish are cast way out from the boats. Some of them are walls of netting up to 100 km long and they're attached to the sea floor by thousands of hooks and traps. So many whales and dolphins get caught in them and then they can't get back up to the surface to breathe. Or they get trapped and starve. If you want to do something, you can get involved in beach clean-ups to help remove this rubbish from our beaches. You can also make posters to let other people know about the dangers."

"You can raise money to support the work of organisations like Whale and Dolphin Conservation too," I chip in.

"So there's a lot that listeners can do to help," the presenter says, taking over again. But I haven't said enough about Angus and I jump back in.

"The whale we rescued is called Angus. We don't know how long he was trapped for but if we hadn't cut the ropes from him, he would have died." I feel my chest tighten at the thought.

"W-what I'm trying to say is that Angus has a family," I go on. "Whales are very intelligent creatures. They speak to each other and care for each other, and they need us to care for them too."

"It's the same as looking out for someone close to you," continues Satchen. "Your help will make a massive difference."

"Thank you, Tulsi and Satchen, the heroes of our story," says the presenter. "Let's give them a big cheer."

After the reporters and everyone else has left, our parents lay out a picnic blanket. We dive into the food that's spread before us.

"Well, you certainly got the whales some attention," says Satchen's dad.

"It was a foolish thing to do, trying to save the whale by yourselves," his mum tells us. I can see the memory of it clouding her eyes. "You were both lucky you didn't drown."

"We're sorry for making you worry," I say. "But we saved Angus and he saved us."

"It's about looking out for each other," says Satchen. "If we all look after the planet, it will look after us."

"No more rowing out to sea," says Mum. "Anything you do from now on can be from the safety of firm ground."

*

One evening later in the summer holidays, Satchen and I arrange to meet again on the

Craig. It's a clear warm night and the faint stars are sprinkled above us like a magical halo.

I tilt my head back to look at the sky.

In a sudden burst of colour, the sky lights up.

"Wow! It's the Northern Lights," says Satchen, his face filled with awe.

Greens, blues and flashes of white swirl in a spectacular display above us.

"It's like fireworks," I say. I feel a tear smudge my cheek but today it's a tear of happiness for Angus and his family. A tear of happiness for the planet because however bad things might seem, there's always something we can do if we stick together.

"We actually saved him," I whisper.

This moment is so precious I want to hold it like a priceless jewel in my memory. I want to

remember everything about our adventure. The terrible exhaustion, the ice-cold sea and how Satchen and I couldn't have done it without each other. I feel so happy being out on the Craig now, in the wilds with nature. I'm determined to do my best to make things better.

"Do you remember the song?" I ask.

"The whale song you mean?" Satchen says.

"It was so strong in the sea when we were with Angus," I say, "like it was echoing inside my whole body. I think it will stay with me for ever."

We link arms under the magical sky and imagine the whale song again. It's loud and fills every inch of space in my little world.

"When we were floating in the sea during the storm," I say, "I felt so close to Angus. It was like there was a bond between us. Like the connection between you and me, you know?

Like sometimes we don't have to say anything because we just know what the other's thinking. Do you think Angus will remember us?"

"Whales are intelligent creatures, so maybe," replies Satchen.

I stare out across the calm blue sea. "Where do you think Angus is now?" I ask.

"I think he's swimming with his family, enjoying the freedom of the waters."

"I think so too," I say. "And maybe one day he'll tell his own babies about the day he was saved by Tulsi and Satchen, the guardians of the whales."